STAR WARS ®

THE POWER OF MYTH

Braided hair

Throwing spear

Woven cloak

Broad sword

FIONN

Double-edged
blade

STAR WARS ®

THE POWER OF MYTH

Activator

Control lock

*Blade
projection
plate*

*Fish-tail
pommel*

SHINING SWORD

**DARTH MAUL'S
LIGHTSABER**

AENEAS

Gothic-style helmet

Dark Sith robe

*Early Roman
shield*

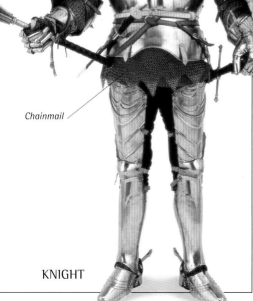

Chainmail

LUCAS
BOOKS

DK

DORLING KINDERSLEY
A DK Publishing Book

DARTH MAUL

KNIGHT

CONTENTS

Traditional Tatooine sand symbols

ANAKIN'S AMULET

Power diversion display

Power delivery gauges

N1-STARFIGHTER READ-OUTS

Orientation grids

Holder for horsehair crest

LEGIONARY HELMET

Strong folded steel

SAMURAI SWORDS

THOR'S HAMMER

Charging port

QUI-GON JINN'S LIGHTSABER

INTRODUCTION

Every civilization on Earth has told mythic stories to express its aspirations, achievements, and the deeper meaning of life. From the earliest times, myths have excited and inspired us because they serve to describe the human experience. Myths show us what we are capable of as individuals.

The *Star Wars* Classic trilogy has come to represent one of the great mythic stories of our time. Luke Skywalker's adventure, starting from his farmboy beginnings and ending with the fulfillment of his spiritual quest to become a Jedi knight, is a hero's journey that speaks to the modern age.

George Lucas, *Star Wars'* creator, has dramatized the saga of an epic struggle between good and evil in a universe complete with its own cultures, languages, landscapes, and heroes. Contemporary characters enact a mythic drama. Swords, sorcery, and chivalry combine with hyperspace travel, blaster weaponry, and droids. Now, with the release of *The Phantom Menace*, the first episode in the *Star Wars* saga, we can discover more of the mythical dynamics of the *Star Wars* universe.

MYTHIC HEROES

The stories of heroes have always had a universal appeal because they are at once ancient and timeless. Every hero has a quest, but before he can achieve his heart's desire he has to complete difficult tasks or fight seemingly impossible battles. Often an evil force must be overcome, or the hero has to learn a new kind of knowledge in order to increase his power. His struggles teach us about our own human potential. In the Star Wars Classic saga, Luke Skywalker is a hero for all time.

WILHELM TELL

Swiss hero Wilhelm Tell was an expert hunter with the crossbow. When the Swiss peasants were humiliated by Austrian soldiers, Wilhelm Tell stood defiant and was arrested. As punishment, Tell was ordered to shoot an apple from the head of his own son with his crossbow. A superb shot, he hit the apple but was ordered to the dungeons. Tell escaped and the ensuing uprising led to Switzerland's independence.

Throwing spear

Magical hood of invisibility

Quiver of bolts

Sword called Balmung

Battle-scarred shield

Woven cloak

Fafnir the dragon

FIONN

Aged seven, the Irish hero Fionn MacCumhaill received the gift of knowledge after burning his finger on a magical salmon he had cooked. When a grown man, Fionn killed a terrifying phantom and in gratitude was made leader of the High King's warriors, called the Fianna.

SIEGFRIED

The German hero Siegfried killed a huge dragon using his great sword Balmung and a magical hood, which made him invisible. After bathing in the dragon's blood, he became invincible, except for a point between his shoulders. This was his weak spot. Siegfried won tremendous victories, but he was stabbed in a family quarrel by an uncle who knew his one weakness.

Thor's hammer was called Mjollnir

THOR

Thor was a mighty Norse warrior god with a thick, red beard and a huge appetite. He was a fighter of giants and monsters, and his most famous weapon was a hammer, which, when thrown, always returned to his hand. He defeated the giant Hrungnir with this hammer. In battle, he wore a belt of goathair, which gave him more strength when tightened.

KING ARTHUR

Raised and educated by the wizard Merlin, Arthur became King of Britain after drawing a sword out of an anvil. Later, he was given a mightier sword named Excalibur by a fairy hand that emerged from a lake. He married Guinevere and organized his knights into the fellowship of the Round Table. When Mordred, Arthur's nephew, tried to seize power, there was a terrible battle. Mordred was slain, but the kingdom was ruined. Arthur ordered Excalibur to be returned to the lake. His body was taken to the mystical isle of Avalon.

THE ARTHURIAN LEGEND

The real Arthur is thought to have been a warlord who lived in Britain around 550 AD and fought against the invading Saxons and Angles. This is how he may have looked. In medieval tellings he is often pictured wearing a glittering suit of armor. His story has become a legend.

Roman-style cloak

Excalibur

Helmet with bear crest

Short slashing sword

Celtic battle shield and sacred symbol

Central metal boss

Laced leather sandals

AENEAS

The Roman hero Aeneas escaped from the besieged city of Troy and, after seven years of adventures, reached Italy. Visiting the underworld, he met his father and learned that his destiny was to rule Rome. He returned to the world, and won the beautiful Lavinia's hand in marriage by slaying her betrothed, a warrior called Turnus. Aeneas became the first king of Rome.

Warrior shield

Protective leg armor

Short sword

JAIME

Jaime was a boy-king raised by the Knights Templar in Spain. He grew up strong and wise, leading his men to take two castles when only 12 years old. From the age of 20 he fought many astute and brilliant campaigns, eventually winning the whole of Valencia from the Moor invaders, and becoming known as "Jaime the Conqueror." He patiently strove to unite his people, who were divided by a continual civil war.

Helmet with cross of St. James

Broadsword

Mace

Cross of the Crusaders

Undergarment

Leg armor

Chainmail

VIRIATO

Viriato was a shepherd who became a skilled horseman and swordsman, leading a general revolt by the Lusitani people against the Romans. He defeated several Roman armies, often by pretending to flee and then outflanking the enemy. After trapping a huge Roman legion, he gained the independence of the Lusitani.

Curved sword is called a "falcata".

Breastplate

TIJL

Tijl Uelenspiegel was a Flemish peasant who used his quick wit and tricks to outwit his people's oppressors, the Spanish overlords who had executed his family. An expert gunner and hand-to-hand fighter, when the Belgian people rebelled, Tijl became their leader.

ROLAND

The Frankish hero Roland was raised in poverty, yet at the age of 15 he became the Emperor Charlemagne's champion. Roland fought the Saracens in Spain for seven years before they asked for peace. As Roland and his army were withdrawing, a huge Saracen force attacked. Roland turned and fought bravely to the end.

Roland blows his horn to warn Charlemagne

LUKE SKYWALKER

The adventure of Luke Skywalker follows the classic stages of a hero's journey. A farm boy from the backwater planet of Tatooine, Luke is pulled from obscurity into a world of adventure when two unusual droids appear in his life carrying a hidden message from a mysterious princess. With the aid of a wise guide, Obi-Wan Kenobi, Luke gains a mystical knowledge of the Force, enlists rugged new companions, Han Solo and Chewbacca, and crosses the galaxy to find the princess.

Chest pack straps

Pressurized g-suit

Life support unit

Alliance symbol

Equipment pocket

THE CALL TO ADVENTURE

In myth, the hero's journey begins with a call to adventure, the first incident on a dangerous path that will separate him from his home and family. The call usually comes in the form of a herald, who carries a message that causes the adventure to begin. Often the hero does not recognize the hand of fate at work, and an event which may seem ordinary is in fact a turning point that catapults the hero into a world of danger and excitement.

Tatooine farm tunic

Sandproof leg bindings

Luke is a poor farm boy who lives on the desert world of Tatooine. Unhappy with a life of farm work, he dreams of distant worlds and a life full of action and challenge.

Garage roof   Entrance dome   Salt flats   Courtyard

Cistern cap | Moisture vaporator extracts water vapor from air | Fusion generator supply tanks

In many myths, the hero appears to be from humble origins. Luke lives with his foster parents, aunt Beru and uncle Owen, on a farm concealed beneath the desert of Tatooine to escape the heat. They have raised him to believe his father was a navigator on a freighter. Not until his journey begins does he learn more of his real identity.

Luke is amazed to find hidden in R2-D2 a cryptic message from a beautiful princess, appealing to the mysterious Obi-Wan Kenobi for help. In a galaxy where droids are generally abused and derided, Luke is kind to the little messenger who has heralded the start of his hero journey.

Aunt Beru Lars   Uncle Owen Lars

DROID HERALDS

Luke aspires to become a space pilot, but is torn between his desire to enroll in the Academy and his loyalty to his family, who need him on the farm and fear that he will never return if he leaves. Luke's life is transformed when his uncle buys the droids C-3PO and R2-D2 from passing Jawas. Their arrival heralds the beginning of the quest that enables Luke to discover his true birthright and destiny.

THE CHILD IS FATHER TO THE MAN

Many years before Luke is born, the life of his father, Anakin, is transformed forever when a beautiful woman walks into his master's junk shop on Tatooine. Her fateful arrival heralds his liberation from slavery and sets him on his own quest.

THE WISE GUIDE

The hero is often unaware of his destiny, but even when he discovers it, he may try to refuse his difficult quest until a wise guide shows him the way. Obi-Wan Kenobi fulfills this role for Luke, giving him advice, Jedi training, and the mystical knowledge of the Force that he will need on his adventure. The path ahead will contain many obstacles to test the hero's skills and courage, but with Obi-Wan's help, Luke takes on the challenge.

Young Luke resembles other mythological heroes when he resists Obi-Wan's call to join him on an adventure. At first he is thinking of his duties on his uncle's farm, until he discovers that his family has been killed by stormtroopers. With nothing left for him on his home world, Luke accompanies Obi-Wan on the trip to Mos Eisley spaceport, and the adventure begins.

Obi-Wan gives Luke a goal and a sense of destiny; he interprets the princess's message and tells Luke that his father was really a starpilot and a Jedi Kinght. Luke now begins to realize his calling: to become a Jedi like his father.

The oracle spoke through a medium called the Sibyl

DIVINE ORACLE
The Greek hero Cadmus had a wise guide in the form of the oracle at Delphi, where the advice of the god Apollo was revealed. It told him where to establish the city of Thebes.

Jedi robes

Hooded cloak

MERLIN

In most myths, the hero loses his wise guide before completing his quest, forcing him to develop his own abilities. In Arthurian legend, the magician Merlin tells Arthur of his destiny to unite the kingdom, and uses his magic and wisdom to help the young king. Then Merlin vanishes, but invisibly continues to counsel Arthur in times of peril. Struck down by Darth Vader on the Death Star, Obi-Wan disappears. Although no longer a physical presence, the Jedi Master, like Merlin, watches over Luke, appearing to inspire him at crucial moments.

YOUNG JEDI
In his younger years, Obi-Wan Kenobi was a great warrior of the Old Republic.

THE MAGIC TALISMAN

In mythology, the wise guide often gives the hero a magical talisman or amulet to guard and assist him on his chosen path. The idea of a magical sword appears many times in legend: it is a powerful symbol that gives the bearer the right to challenge authority. Obi-Wan gives Luke his Jedi father's lightsaber.

THOR'S HAMMER
In Norse legend, the god Thor's magic talisman was a mighty hammer called Mjollnir. The Vikings believed thunder was the sound of Thor's hammer blows in battle.

By accepting the lightsaber from his wise guide Obi-Wan Kenobi, Luke continues his father's Jedi heritage. The weapon is a powerful talisman, which inspires him to take the first step on his path toward Jedi knighthood.

Jerba leather cord

Japor ivory wood snippet obtained by Anakin through trading.

ANAKIN'S AMULET
Knowing that the future is uncertain, the boy Anakin Skywalker carves this good-luck talisman for his friend Padmé. He hopes that she will remember him by this token.

Traditional Tattooine sand symbols

DRAGON-SLAYER
The hero Siegfried (Sigurd) reforges his father Sigmund's sword after it is broken by Odin, the god of battles. In doing so he is able to continue his father's heroic deeds. The sword gives Siegfried such strength that he kills the dragon Fafnir and becomes invincible in battle.

EXCALIBUR
King Arthur was handed the sacred sword Excalibur by the mysterious Lady of the Lake. It became a symbol of his kingship and power.

SWORDS OF POWER
The Arthurian romances of the Middle Ages envisage Excalibur as a great and shining sword like this one (*left*), which was made for a rich knight in the 15th century. Elaborate sword hilts (*right*) were a sign of the owner's wealth and status.

HERO PARTNERS

The hero may begin his journey alone, but he soon meets "hero partners" who will accompany him on his adventure. Luke finds his future companions in the sleazy Mos Eisley cantina, a drinking hole for space pirates, smugglers, and fugitives of every species in the galaxy.

Luke's trusty friends are an unusual bunch: a huge Wookiee, a mercenary, two droids, and a princess.

CHEWBACCA

Captain Solo's first mate is the imposing eight-foot (2.22-m) tall Wookiee, Chewbacca. Rescued from slavery by Han Solo, Chewie has become his lifelong friend and has risked his life for Solo on many occasions.

Han Solo's reputation as a gunfighter matches his renown as captain of the *Falcon*. Between Solo's fast draw and Chewbacca's tremendous strength, the two make a formidable team.

Focused expression

HAN SOLO

Mercenary pilot, smuggler, and fastest draw in the galaxy, Han Solo is a rugged individual of the Galactic Rim. A Corellian pilot of the finest caliber, Solo is also a gambler. He gained control of his destiny when he won his ship from Lando Calrissian in the best game of sabacc he ever played. Sometimes reckless and foolhardy, Solo is also courageous and daring.

Spacer's waistcoat

Corelllian blood stripe

HONORABLE KNIGHTS

King Arthur's companions and defenders were the Knights of the Round Table, who met at Camelot. Each knight swore, on pain of death, to be loyal to the king, to be merciful, to defend women, and never to fight for any wrongful cause.

Jason *The Golden Fleece* *Medea*

JAR JAR BINKS

Rescued by the Jedi Qui-Gon Jinn during the invasion of Naboo, Jar Jar Binks feels honor bound to be the Jedi's companion for life. At first, Qui-Gon is not pleased by the Gungan's company, but gradually he realizes that the amphibian is a valuable ally.

MILLENNIUM FALCON

Han Solo's Corellian pirate ship has had certain modifications to its hyperdrive system that make it one of the fastest spaceships in the galaxy. The *Falcon* also has heavy-duty weapons.

JASON AND THE ARGONAUTS

The Greek hero Jason was assisted by the most famous traveling companions in mythology, including the hero Hercules. In a ship called the *Argo*, they set sail on a mission to capture a fabulous treasure known as the Golden Fleece. Medea was a princess who fell in love with Jason and helped him obtain the Fleece.

RESCUING THE PRINCESS

Entering a labyrinth, or a doorway into the unknown, is often an obstacle the hero must overcome in the course of his journey. When Luke and his companions come out of hyperspace expecting to find Alderaan, their ship is sucked toward the Death Star, a colossal Imperial battle station. Inside, they must negotiate a soulless maze of dimly lit chambers, corridors, and shafts. By chance, Luke discovers that the princess is being held captive here.

The Death Star is a modern, high-tech labyrinth with a force of evil at its center. It annihilates its enemies with incredible firepower.

Like many mythological heroes, Luke and Han Solo must find a way through the maze. Dressed in stolen Imperial armor they find the princess's cell.

Leia's rescuers

Leia reveals nothing of the Rebels' whereabouts to Darth Vader. Alone in her cell, she does not expect to be rescued from her impending execution. Luke's arrival is at first a disappointment to her; dressed in armor, she takes him for a rather short stormtrooper!

Like the mythological dragon who guards the treasure or the damsel, Darth Vader holds Princess Leia captive in the center of the vast Death Star.

Having found the princess, Luke and Han must now try to escape the legions of stormtroopers closing in on them at every turn. Their only hope is that Obi-Wan Kenobi has succeeded in deactivating the tractor beam which drew them aboard.

MONSTERS IN THE MAZE

Mazes in myths often come with nasty surprises lurking around the corner. The Greek hero Theseus found his way through a labyrinth to the lair of the Minotaur, a flesh-eating monster that was part bull, part man. After killing the beast in combat, Theseus made his way out by following the trail of thread he had left on entering. Similarly, Luke and his companions meet a sewer-dwelling dianoga deep in the bowels of the Death Star. Luke is lucky to escape with his life.

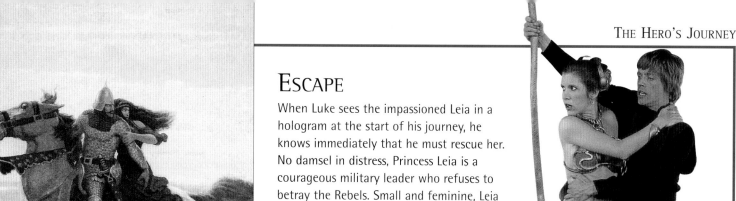

ESCAPE

When Luke sees the impassioned Leia in a hologram at the start of his journey, he knows immediately that he must rescue her. No damsel in distress, Princess Leia is a courageous military leader who refuses to betray the Rebels. Small and feminine, Leia embodies the forces of good. She is the extreme opposite of her captor, Darth Vader, who is powerful, ruthless, and in his skull-like mask and black robes, represents the forces of evil.

SIR LANCELOT TO THE RESCUE

Lancelot was King Arthur's greatest knight. One of his bravest deeds was to rescue the princess Elaine from a tower on fire, so lifting a witch's curse on the kingdom.

Later, Leia is captured once more, this time by Jabba the Hutt. Luke again comes to her rescue, heroically sweeping her from Jabba's sail barge.

PERSEUS

After slaying the Medusa, the Greek hero Perseus found a princess chained to a rock in sacrifice to a sea-dragon. As the beast emerged, Perseus brandished Medusa's head, and its gaze turned the monster to stone.

As Luke attacks Jabba's guards, Leia seizes her chance, breaks free, and strangles her captor with her slave chains.

EVIL AT THE HEART OF THE LABYRINTH

In former years, the galactic capital, Corucsant, was the labyrinthine hiding place of the unseen Sith, a dark order plotting the Old Republic's downfall in its time of weakness. This phantom menace radiates outward from the core, drawing into its dark web individuals and worlds far beyond Coruscant.

Darth Sidious is the monster at the heart of this labyrinth. His power extends far into the government.

An entire world enveloped by a single city, trillions inhabit the city of Coruscant.

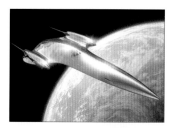

Queen Amidala is saved from an invasion when two Jedi Knights come to her rescue. They escape in the Queen's Royal Starship.

HERO ACTION

In myth, the hero's battle is often against a powerful enemy in the form of an enormous beast, which either guards a prize or threatens the hero's people. The gods in Greek legends looked kindly on mortals who showed courage when fighting monsters and would find ways of helping. Likewise, the Force aids Luke in his hero deeds. His small fighter craft is insignificant compared with the gigantic Death Star or a colossal Imperial Walker, but with courage, skill, and faith in the Force, he destroys them.

During the battle of Hoth, Luke is shot down and just manages to struggle out of his cockpit before his snowspeeder is crushed by a giant AT-AT. Never giving up, Luke fires his harpoon at the vehicle's undercarriage and hoists himself up, throwing a thermal detonator into the walker's hatch.

JEDI BLADE

In the best tradition of heroic action, Luke's swordlike weapon means he must confront his enemies at very close quarters. Like many swords in myth, the Jedi lightsaber imparts a superhuman strength to the hero, from which opponents must flee or die.

LEGBOUND
Luke brings an AT-AT crashing to the snow by entangling its legs with his snowspeeder tow cable – a victory of courage over brute strength.

Attacking stance

BEASTLY STRENGTH
At Nemea, there lived a lion with skin so tough no weapon could pierce it. The hero Hercules made a massive club, beat the lion, and strangled it. He used the beast's sharp claws to skin it, and wore the hide for his protection.

Fafnir the dragon

The shining sword "Balmung" pierces Fafnir's heart.

Siegfried

SIEGFRIED THE FEARLESS
Siegfied's guardian, an evil dwarf, led him to the lair of the terrifying dragon Fafnir, who guarded a hoard of gold. Awoken, Fafnir was shocked by Siegfried's complete lack of fear, and was too slow to avoid the boy's deadly blow.

Grendel's mother   *Beowulf*

In true hero style, Luke jams open the Rancor's mouth with a bone, before trapping its head under a portcullis, killing it.

BEOWULF
Beowulf became a hero by killing Grendel, the monster that had been attacking the Danish court for 12 years. Then Grendel's mother arrived to take revenge for her son. Beowulf swam to the bottom of the creature's lake to face her. His followers thought he was dead, but he emerged from the bloodied waters holding up his sword and the monster's head.

MONSTER COMBAT
Heroes in myth invariably do battle with evil, nightmarish monsters during their quest. Luke shows no terror when he faces the Rancor beast without his lightsaber, and narrowly avoids being devoured by using his wit and agility.

WAMPA DINNER
Knocked unconscious by this ice creature on Hoth, Luke is dragged back to its gory lair. Using the Force, he is just able to grab his lightsaber before he becomes its next meal!

X-WING ATTACK
In his X-wing fighter, Luke uses the Force to guide a proton torpedo into the Death Star's exhaust port—a tiny target. The resulting destruction of this giant, technological monster is a major Rebel victory.

ACCIDENTAL HERO
Anakin's dreams come true faster than he could ever imagine when he finds himself hiding in the cockpit of a Naboo starfighter. The autopilot engages and he flies into the heart of the battle raging above. Anakin must learn the controls furiously fast before he is killed. He is saved by his heroic courage and his natural aptitude as a pilot.

Crash-landing deep within the Droid Control Ship, Anakin accidentally fires his torpedoes into the pilot reactors, setting off a cataclysmic chain reaction.

THE SACRED GROVE

In myth, one of the trials of the hero is to leave the world behind and go alone into a forest full of danger and sorcery. Only here will he receive knowledge that transforms and aids him on his quest. On Obi-Wan's advice, Luke travels to the planet Dagobah to be trained by the Jedi Master Yoda. In Dagobah's forests, Luke gains a deeper understanding of the Force and of himself.

CAVE OF EVIL

The forest is also a symbol for the unconscious mind, which is full of dark and hidden emotions. At Yoda's bidding, Luke enters a cave that is "strong with the dark side." Here he must confront his own character alone and discovers that his first enemy is, in fact, himself and his own dark side. Only when he has conquered this will he be able to confront the might of Darth Vader.

Dagobah is covered with immense, gnarled trees. Many cultures hold trees sacred and believe them to have certain magical energies and powers.

TREE SPIRITS

In ancient Europe, druids worshipped the Celtic gods beneath holy oaks. Evil spirits were believed to roam the groves after sunset and many were terrified to enter.

Blade activated in anticipation

YODA'S DWELLING

Like the woodmen in fairy stories, Yoda lives humbly, but he is a master of the powers of nature and of the power deep within himself. He hopes to pass on this knowledge to Luke but despairs of the boy's impatience.

SANCTUARY

The forest also afforded protection for those fleeing authority. Robin Hood and his men raided the king's barons from the safety and camouflage of the Sherwood Forest.

Luke learns something of the nature of the Force when he discovers that Yoda is not the mighty warrior he had supposed, but a diminutive, patient, and unassuming individual.

THE MYSTICAL UNION

An important stage of the hero's journey is a mystical union with a woman. First though, the hero must prove himself worthy of her. After meeting Princess Leia, Han Solo begins his own hero journey, and is gradually transformed from a selfish individual to a compassionate fighter for the Rebellion. Luke's hero quest is a spiritual one; Han's is to become a lover.

FATAL ATTRACTION

The knight Tristan and a king's bride, Iseult, fell deeply in love with each other after unknowingly drinking a cup of magic potion. Iseult married the king and Tristan another woman. Wounded in battle, Tristan sent for Iseult, but his jealous wife falsely told him she was not coming. The knight died in despair.

At first, Han and Leia seem an unlikely match. She is a high-born princess and he is an outlaw. Typical of a modern romance, there is no love at first sight. When they first meet, Leia thinks Han is stupid and selfish. Han thinks her demanding and self-important.

Siegfried is often depicted with blond, curly hair.

ANAKIN AND PADMÉ

Although still only a child, when Anakin Skywalker first sets eyes on the beautiful Padmé, he is captivated and strongly drawn to her. Giving her a lucky charm to remember him by, Anakin longs to meet her and be with her again.

LANCELOT'S FORBIDDEN LOVE

In the Arthurian legends, Sir Lancelot secretly fell in love with Guinevere, King Arthur's beloved queen. Although they both fought their feelings for each other, their love was preordained. Lancelot was punished by being denied the Holy Grail after years of searching for it. When Arthur died, Guinevere went into seclusion and Lancelot entered a hermitage.

Despite trading frequent insults, the love between Han and Leia grows. Before they are separated on Cloud City, Leia finally affirms her love to him.

GERMAN ROMANCE

In one version of Siegfried's story, the hero finds Brunhild asleep on a rock surrounded by fire. Brunhild was a Valkyrie, a warrior maiden, and a daughter of the Norse god Odin. Siegfried awakens her with a kiss and the two fall in love, pledging their loyalty to each other forever.

SACRIFICE AND BETRAYAL

O n his journey, the hero must often make a sacrifice in return for gaining knowledge and mystical insight—in Luke's case, this knowledge is the realization that the dark side within himself is represented by his own father, Darth Vader. On Han's journey, there is betrayal and the discovery that Leia loves him. But before he can return her love, he must endure a kind of "death" and be frozen in carbonite for transportation to the lair of Jabba the Hutt.

Luke is drawn to Cloud City by a vision of his friends Leia and Han in danger. It represents a turning point in the lives of all three.

Luke is lured into the hellish depths of Cloud City to meet his own personal nemesis. Here he encounters the evil Darth Vader and in close combat discovers the hideous truth of his identity.

CONFRONTATION AND DENIAL

Luke confronts Vader on Cloud City and loses his hand in the battle that ensues. His father entreats Luke to join him or die. Realizing that his father represents everything that he despises, Luke would prefer to die than become a force for evil. Rather than yield to his father's will, the hero chooses to sacrifice his life and leaps into the abyss.

Sluglike in appearance, crime lord Jabba the Hutt doesn't forget old debts. He posts a bounty on Han's head—and Boba Fett is collecting.

Helmet hides identity

Jet backpack with rocket launcher

Utility pouch

BOBA FETT
A mysterious but fanatical bounty hunter with his own code of honor, Boba Fett wears a suit of battle armor from another era.

Loki, the jealous god

Mistletoe spear

Hoder, Balder's blind brother, innocently throws the spear.

FERRYMAN TO HELL

In Greek mythology, the dead had to cross the river Styx to reach the underworld, and were taken by a ferryman, Charon, who always had to be paid.

Against a doom-laden sky, Boba Fett now ferries his precious bounty, Han's carbon-frozen body, to the underworld of Jabba's palace.

CAST IN CARBONITE

An evil power that can turn someone to stone is found in many myths. It is death but not death, which leaves the possibility that it can be reversed. Here, Han has been turned into a block of carbonite. Normally used as a way of bonding condensed Tibanna gas for transport, it can be used to keep life forms in suspended animation—as long as the painful freezing process does not kill them first.

Carbon-freezing is a very painful experience

A FRIEND DECEIVED

Having betrayed Han to Darth Vader, Lando Calrissian guiltily looks at his friend, who has been tortured and frozen in carbonite. Lando's guilt will eventually lead to his redemption, when he joins the Rebels' cause.

Balder—the god beloved by all

Balder is slain by the mistletoe spear.

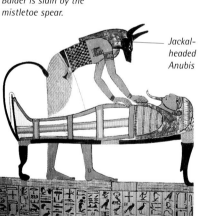

Jackal-headed Anubis

BALDER'S BETRAYER

In a famous Norse myth, the god Loki was jealous when he heard that everything in creation had vowed never to harm the handsome god Balder. Discovering that mistletoe had not been included, Loki persuaded Balder's brother, the blind god Hoder, to throw a mistletoe spear at Balder, which killed him.

PRESERVING THE BODY

Like Han being frozen for Boba Fett's journey, bodies in ancient Egypt were prepared for a life beyond the stars by the process of embalming. Anubis was the jackal-headed god of this ancient art.

RETURN OF THE HERO

The hero is ready to return home when he has proved his worth through brave action and dangerous trials. Luke has rescued the princess, destroyed the Death Star, and learned the ways of the Force. In mythology, the hero must now use his knowledge to benefit his people. Returning home to Tatooine, Luke's first act is to rescue Han from Jabba the Hutt.

JEDI KNIGHT

Back on Tatooine, Luke appears for the first time wearing the simple robes of the Jedi order, a sign that he has achieved his spiritual quest: to become a Jedi Knight.

THE RETURN OF ODYSSEUS

Trying to return home from the Trojan Wars, the Greek hero Odysseus had many dangerous adventures. His ship was constantly blown off course because he had offended the sea god, Poseidon.

Odysseus finally made it home after 20 years. His wife, Penelope, had waited faithfully for his return, never believing that he was dead. She had resisted the many suitors who wanted to marry her and take Odysseus's place.

To rescue Han, Luke must enter the palace of the odious Hutt, Jabba. This is another labyrinth with a monster at the core.

Joseph tells his brothers who he is, and forgives them

JOSEPH REVEALS HIS IDENTITY TO HIS BROTHERS

In this famous Bible story, a boy called Joseph is sold into slavery by his brothers. Many years later, when he has risen to become a powerful minister in Egypt, a terrible famine occurs, and Joseph's brothers come to plead before him for grain. He reveals his identity to them and they are amazed and ashamed. Joseph returns to their lives, and having experienced God's love, forgives them.

FAMILY REUNION

Inside the palace Luke finds Leia enslaved by Jabba. He is also returning to his family, for by now he has sensed that Leia is his sister.

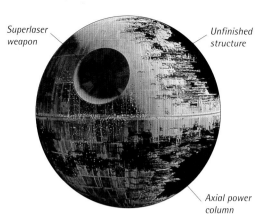

Superlaser weapon

Unfinished structure

Axial power column

DESCENT TO THE UNDERWORLD

Having returned home, the hero is ready to visit the underworld, either to accomplish a heroic task, as with Hercules, or to understand more of the world, like Aeneas. Luke must enter the dark underworld of the second Death Star to save the side of his father, Darth Vader, that he senses is still good.

The Emperor's dark throne room recalls the gloom of the underworld in Greek mythology, where Hades held his court.

THE SECOND DEATH STAR

The Emperor conceived the second Death Star as a colossal trap, which would use a false image of vulnerability to lure the Rebel fleet into combat. He almost succeeded, but never considered that the heroism of Luke's friends would succeed in disabling the battle station's protective shields.

Before Luke can redeem his father, he must face the dark side's most powerful figure, the Emperor himself. The tyrant sits on a throne which is framed by a web-shaped window. Spiderlike, he awaits the Rebellion's destruction and Luke's conversion.

Enraged at his failure to recruit Luke to the dark side of the Force, the Emperor slowly electrocutes the hero with Force lightning. The moment for Darth Vader to help his son has finally come.

On Cloud City, the fiery glow and sulphurous gases of the Carbon Freezing Chamber make it a kind of underworld. Luke is led to this hellish place to face Vader.

Hercules enters the underworld

UNDERWATER WORLD

The Jedi Obi-Wan Kenobi and Qui-Gon Jinn descend beneath the lakes of Naboo to travel through the planet's core. Monstrous sea creatures lurk in these dangerous depths, waiting to prey on anything that swims.

HERCULES IN HELL

The hero Hercules became a god by performing 12 tasks. The twelfth was the hardest. He had bring back the three-headed watchdog of hell, Cerberus. Hercules was greeted by Hades himself, who laughed and said, "The dog is yours if you can take him." The hero throttled it with his huge arms and dragged it up to the world of day.

Persephone

Anchises, the spirit of Aeneas's father

RECONCILIATION WITH THE FATHER

On his long journey, the mythical hero sometimes needs to make amends with his father to achieve completion. When Luke refuses to kill his father at the Emperor's bidding, the Emperor is enraged and turns on him. Helpless, Luke appeals to his father for help. This is Darth Vader's moment to find the good in himself. After an agonizing few seconds of hesitation, Vader's good side wins over the evil. He redeems himself by saving Luke and destroying the Emperor, but it is at the cost of his own life.

Darth Vader kills his master by casting him down a core shaft on the second Death Star. The Emperor's death is marked by an immense explosion of Force lightning.

THE FATHER'S PROPHECY

The Roman hero Aeneas longed to see his dead father Anchises once more. Taking a golden branch as an offering for Persephone, queen of the underworld, he went in search of him. Seeing Anchises's spirit, Aeneas tried to embrace him, but found himself grasping the air. They could talk, however, and Anchises amazed his son by telling him he would become Rome's first king.

Before he can make peace with his father, Luke must prove that he is a match for him in strength and character. In a final epic lightsaber duel, Vader realizes that his son's powers have become greater than his own and falls, beaten.

THE GOOD SON
Sir Lancelot, King Arthur's closest friend, had an illegitimate son, named Galahad. Father and son were reconciled after many years when the Holy Grail was denied Lancelot, but granted to Galahad, who was the purest of all the knights. Galahad and Lancelot are shown here fighting together.

The removal of Vader's mask is symbolic of his release from the dark side of the Force. Luke no longer fears his father and can now see him as a person. In his last moments before dying, Vader gazes lovingly at Luke with his own eyes, not those of his mask. He has turned back to the side of good and shows that, in the end, he has a heart that can be opened by love for his son. Luke now feels at one with his father.

FINAL VICTORY

The hero's journey is over and Luke has attained his quest. The Emperor and the evil that radiated from him have been destroyed, ultimately through an appeal to love – Darth Vader's love for his son. The hero companions, Han, Leia, and Chewie, relax with Luke on the forest moon of Endor as tumultous celebrations break out in cities across the galaxy.

Lilies symbolize the knight's purity | Sir Galahad | The Grail chapel | The Holy Grail

With the Empire destroyed, Luke's adventure ends happily. The spirits of Yoda, Obi-Wan Kenobi, and Anakin Skywalker – no longer Darth Vader – watch the celebrations.

THE END OF THE QUEST

After a journey lasting many years, the brave Sir Galahad freed the land from hunger and misery by finding the Grail castle and the Holy Grail. A symbol of purity and courage, only Galahad was worthy of touching the Grail. The experience was so spiritual that he then no longer wanted to live in the world.

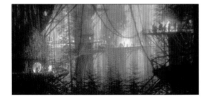

The Empire fell when Luke's friends destroyed the generator on Endor that was maintaining the second Death Star's protective shields. Endor is a world redolent of the mythical enchanted forest.

PURIFYING FLAME

While the Rebels celebrate the Emperor's downfall, Luke burns his father's armor on a ceremonial funeral pyre. In mythology and many religions, fires are believed to purify the soul, setting it free to rise to heaven. For Luke, the victory is the greater because he has won freedom for the galaxy and restored his father's spirit to the good side of the Force. But it is a sad occasion too, since just as he has found his father, he has had to lose him.

As news spreads of the Emperor's death the citizens of the galaxy rejoice and the party lasts for many days and nights.

DEATH OF A HERO

At the end of his great life, the body of the hero Hercules was placed on a funeral pyre. His mortal shade went to wander in the underworld, but his immortal self rose to heaven, where he joined the other gods.

NABOO PARTY

After their triumph over the Trade Federation invasion, the people of Naboo celebrate with a great victory parade.

THE HERO'S SHIPS

Luke Skywalker climbs into the cockpit of an X-wing starfighter in the attack on the first Death Star. In the years afterward, Luke takes this ship into battle and adventure against pirates and imperial ships, bringing many victories for the hard-pressed Rebels. Luke's abilities as a fighter pilot and his legendary vessel, the X-wing fighter, make him one of the great warrior figures in the struggle against the Empire.

The X-wings and TIE fighters attack in combat formation. The different rebel squadrons are assigned a color. Luke's designation is "Red Five".

FOUR-CANNON FIGHTER
The X-wing's four heavy-duty laser generators operate at the limits of safety to create maximum firepower.

The X-wing targeting display provides confirmation of targets within striking range.

T-65 X-WING

Despite its heavy firepower, hyperdrive, and defensive shields, the X-wing starfighter is still maneuvreable enough for close combat with the Empire's lethally agile TIE fighters. Its long-range cannons can engage an oncoming enemy before it can return fire. An on-board astromech droid carries out in-flight repairs.

On-board droid

Life support

Cockpit canopy

Turbo impeller

Hyperdrive

Deflector shield projector

Primary sensor array

Laser firing tip

Communication antenna

Control pedals

Laser cannon mount

Sensor jamming unit

Hydraulic lines

Proton torpedo

Acceleration compensator

Power converters rephase energy for ship subsystems

Power generator

Power coupling

THE COCKPIT
Comprehensive cockpit displays allow the pilot to control energy output throughout the ship's systems during combat.

Magnetic flashback suppressors deflect the occasional unstable laser bolt

Laser cooling sleeve

Laser generator

REBEL SNOWSPEEDER

The Rebels' snowspeeders are equipped with armor plating and heavy-duty laser cannons. Modified to operate in the freezing temperatures of Hoth, they have no defensive shields and must rely on agility and speed in battle. Luke entangles the legs of an attacking Imperial walker with the craft's tow cable.

Blasted out of the sky, Luke struggles out of his cockpit before his snowspeeder is crushed by an AT-AT.

Targeting sensors

Pilot

Gunner

ID markings

Armored canopy

Aft repulsor unit

Harpoon and tow cable

Repulsor generator

Armor plate

Laser generator

Final stage energizer

Laser barrel

Power coupling

Power convertor

Circuitry access

Air intake

Wingtip repulsor projectors

Fuel tank

TIE FIGHTER

During their attack on the Death Star, X-wings encounter deadly TIE fighters, the Empire's main small fighter craft. TIEs are light and very maneuverable because they are built without hyperdrive or shields.

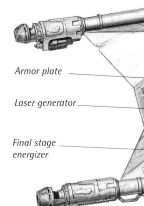

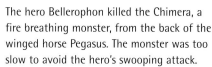

This wartime painting shows Spitfires and Messerschmitts in a battle over London. When a pilot picked up an enemy on his tail, he could sometimes escape by spiraling downward, pretending to be hit.

Powerful X-wings dive on Imperial fighters like legendary winged horses. The TIE fighter's terrifying gas-powered roar recalls the howl of the Chimera encountered by the Greek hero Bellerophon.

The hero Bellerophon killed the Chimera, a fire breathing monster, from the back of the winged horse Pegasus. The monster was too slow to avoid the hero's swooping attack.

Bellerophon

Pegasus

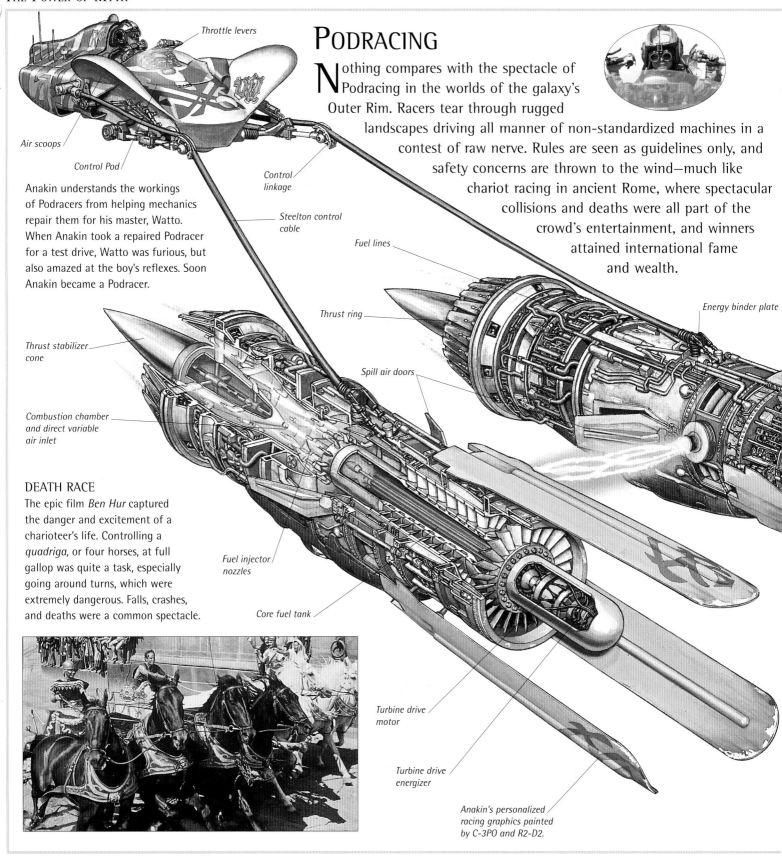

PODRACING

Nothing compares with the spectacle of Podracing in the worlds of the galaxy's Outer Rim. Racers tear through rugged landscapes driving all manner of non-standardized machines in a contest of raw nerve. Rules are seen as guidelines only, and safety concerns are thrown to the wind—much like chariot racing in ancient Rome, where spectacular collisions and deaths were all part of the crowd's entertainment, and winners attained international fame and wealth.

Anakin understands the workings of Podracers from helping mechanics repair them for his master, Watto. When Anakin took a repaired Podracer for a test drive, Watto was furious, but also amazed at the boy's reflexes. Soon Anakin became a Podracer.

Throttle levers

Air scoops

Control Pod

Control linkage

Steelton control cable

Fuel lines

Thrust ring

Energy binder plate

Thrust stabilizer cone

Spill air doors

Combustion chamber and direct variable air inlet

Fuel injector nozzles

Core fuel tank

Turbine drive motor

Turbine drive energizer

Anakin's personalized racing graphics painted by C-3PO and R2-D2.

DEATH RACE
The epic film *Ben Hur* captured the danger and excitement of a charioteer's life. Controlling a *quadriga*, or four horses, at full gallop was quite a task, especially going around turns, which were extremely dangerous. Falls, crashes, and deaths were a common spectacle.

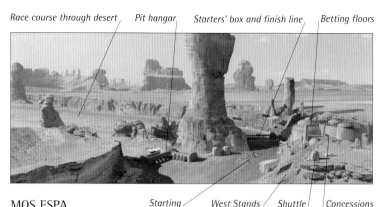

Race course through desert · Pit hangar · Starters' box and finish line · Betting floors

Starting grid · West Stands · Shuttle terminal · Concessions concourse

MOS ESPA
The Mos Espa Arena holds more than 100,000 spectators. The atmosphere before a Podrace is electric. Fans take their seats in the stands, the rich enter their boxes; and the betting floors are scenes of feverish activity as the odds change every few seconds.

People flocked from all over the Roman Empire to watch the chariot races at the Circus Maximus. A day at the races was a day spent betting, cheering, and eating. Fans followed their favorite teams and drivers with the passion of modern football supporters. Sometimes rivalry between fans led to violence.

Primary intake turbine

Imperial box

Fine staturary adorns central concourse

Indicators show the number of laps to go

Starting gates between two towers

Fuel atomizer

Triple air scoops

CIRCUS MAXIMUS
The Circus Maximus in Rome could seat up to 250,000 people. Chariots erupted from the starting gates (between the two towers) and thundered around in a counterclockwise direction. Seven laps later, the survivors crossed the finish line across from the imperial box, on the left.

AND THEY'RE OFF!
At the Mos Espa Arena, Jabba the Hutt opens the race by spitting a gorg's head at a gong. In Rome, the emperor wasn't so crude; he gave the starting sign by dropping a white handkerchief from the imperial box.

Anakin's chief adversary, Sebulba, has reached the top by cheating. His illegal flame emitter fries competitors' engines. Chariot wheels in the Circus Maximus were sometimes equipped with large blades to destroy opponents who got too close.

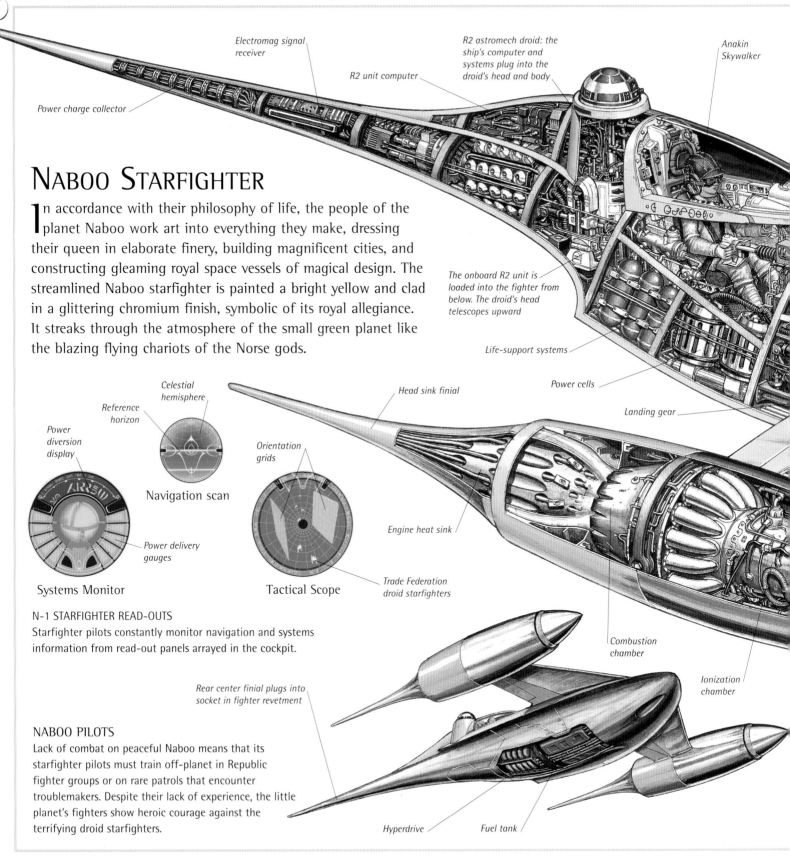

Power charge collector

Electromag signal receiver

R2 unit computer

R2 astromech droid: the ship's computer and systems plug into the droid's head and body

Anakin Skywalker

NABOO STARFIGHTER

In accordance with their philosophy of life, the people of the planet Naboo work art into everything they make, dressing their queen in elaborate finery, building magnificent cities, and constructing gleaming royal space vessels of magical design. The streamlined Naboo starfighter is painted a bright yellow and clad in a glittering chromium finish, symbolic of its royal allegiance. It streaks through the atmosphere of the small green planet like the blazing flying chariots of the Norse gods.

The onboard R2 unit is loaded into the fighter from below. The droid's head telescopes upward

Life-support systems

Power cells

Head sink finial

Landing gear

Power diversion display

Reference horizon

Celestial hemisphere

Orientation grids

Power delivery gauges

Navigation scan

Systems Monitor

Tactical Scope

Trade Federation droid starfighters

Engine heat sink

Combustion chamber

Ionization chamber

N-1 STARFIGHTER READ-OUTS
Starfighter pilots constantly monitor navigation and systems information from read-out panels arrayed in the cockpit.

Rear center finial plugs into socket in fighter revetment

NABOO PILOTS
Lack of combat on peaceful Naboo means that its starfighter pilots must train off-planet in Republic fighter groups or on rare patrols that encounter troublemakers. Despite their lack of experience, the little planet's fighters show heroic courage against the terrifying droid starfighters.

Hyperdrive

Fuel tank

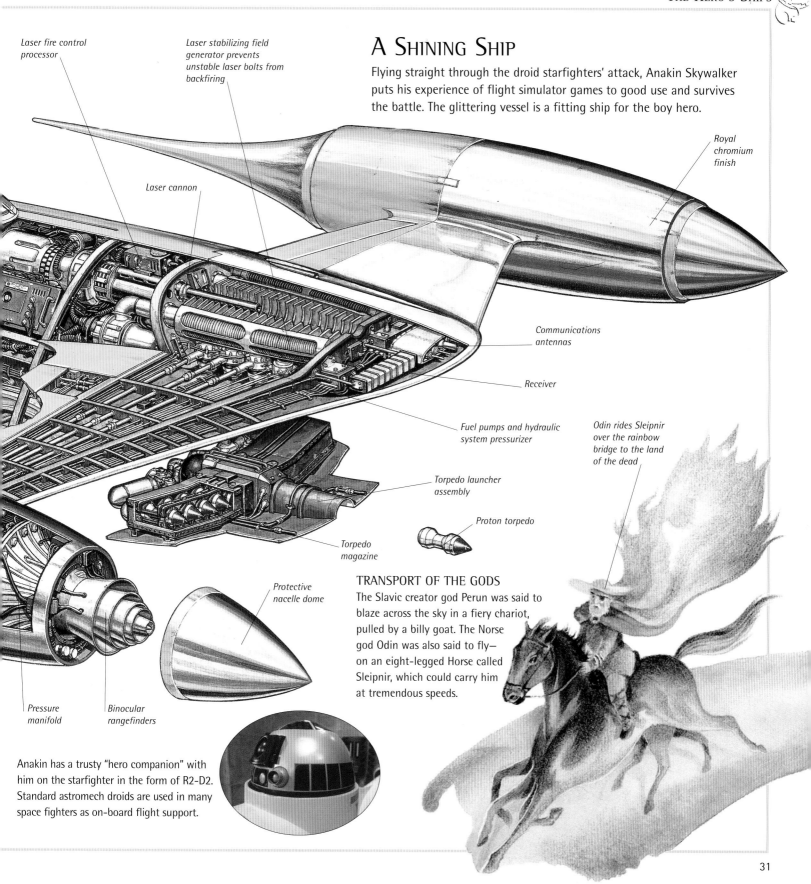

Laser fire control processor

Laser stabilizing field generator prevents unstable laser bolts from backfiring

Laser cannon

A SHINING SHIP

Flying straight through the droid starfighters' attack, Anakin Skywalker puts his experience of flight simulator games to good use and survives the battle. The glittering vessel is a fitting ship for the boy hero.

Royal chromium finish

Communications antennas

Receiver

Fuel pumps and hydraulic system pressurizer

Odin rides Sleipnir over the rainbow bridge to the land of the dead

Torpedo launcher assembly

Proton torpedo

Torpedo magazine

TRANSPORT OF THE GODS

The Slavic creator god Perun was said to blaze across the sky in a fiery chariot, pulled by a billy goat. The Norse god Odin was also said to fly— on an eight-legged Horse called Sleipnir, which could carry him at tremendous speeds.

Protective nacelle dome

Pressure manifold

Binocular rangefinders

Anakin has a trusty "hero companion" with him on the starfighter in the form of R2-D2. Standard astromech droids are used in many space fighters as on-board flight support.

31

JEDI TRAINING

Although tiny in stature, the wise Jedi Master Yoda is very powerful with the Force. His years of contemplation have given him deep insight and extraordinary abilities. One of his greatest challenges is training Luke, who arrives on Dagobah an impatient would-be Jedi. Yoda instills in him the faith, peace, and harmony with the Force that will fulfill the young man's potential and guard him from the dark side. To his final student, Yoda imparts the ancient Jedi traditions that are the galaxy's last hope.

At first, Luke bridles at Yoda's demanding training techniques, but the Jedi Master's profound teachings will guide Luke's path for the rest of his life, and protect him from the dark road of temptation, anger, and evil.

Yoda lives a hermit's life and spends his days in meditation, seeing ever deeper into the infinite tapestry that is the living vitality of the Force.

ZEN BUDDHISM

Jedi philosophy shares similarities with Zen Buddhism, which holds that truth and enlightenment can be found through personal insights and self-mastery. Yoda urges Luke to concentrate, and teaches him to find the still center within, from which he can act with clarity. As with Jedi training, Buddhist knowledge is handed down as an inspiration to students, who are "awakened" by a teacher who has experienced the truth of the teachings.

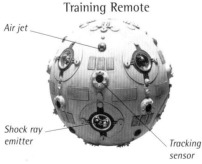

Training Remote

Air jet

Shock ray emitter

Tracking sensor

THE POWER OF THE FORCE

Jedi Knights draw their power from the Force, an omnipresent, subtle energy field surrounding all living things. The Force can lend telekinetic powers and give insight into the future, the past, or the thoughts of others. Luke starts to sense his Force attunement by pitting his lightsaber against this simple remote.

The Buddha finds enlightenment under a Bodhi tree.

TEMPLAR KNIGHTS

In the early days of the crusades, a band of idealistic knights formed a holy warrior order with the aim of protecting pilgrims to the Holy Land. They became known as Templars and differed from other monks by remaining trained fighters. Skilled warriors who joined had to reject the world for a monastic life. They swore to serve the order faithfully and to help those in need.

LUKE SKYWALKER

Luke develops his ability with the Force according to the teachings of his mentors Obi-Wan Kenobi and Yoda. Though he walks his path alone and without fellow initiates, Luke meditates and trains hard to fulfill his destiny and become a Jedi Knight. On Dagobah, Yoda awakens his dormant abilities and Force sensitivity. Focusing his determination, Luke prepares himself for his destined confrontation with Darth Vader, holding in his heart the galaxy's hope for freedom.

Black Jedi clothing

Utility belt

Mechanical hand

Travel boots

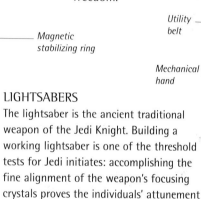

Blade energy channel

Magnetic stabilizing ring

Handgrip

Primary crystal

Diatium power cell

LIGHTSABERS

The lightsaber is the ancient traditional weapon of the Jedi Knight. Building a working lightsaber is one of the threshold tests for Jedi initiates: accomplishing the fine alignment of the weapon's focusing crystals proves the individuals' attunement to the Force. Lightsabers tend to follow a similar basic structure, but are usually customized by their Jedi builders.

MARTIAL ARTS

In Japan, the training of Zen Buddhist monks often combines meditation with fencing, archery, and jujitsu. The martial arts help initiates focus on their spiritual natures, by increasing their self-confidence, assertiveness, and concentration. Learning the martial arts correctly takes many years of hard work. There are many moves the initiates have to perfect.

JEDI DEFENDERS

Jedi Knights use the Force purely for knowledge and defense, never aggression. They are mediators, negotiators, and counselors first of all, and warriors only as a last resort.

QUI-GON JINN

Master Qui-Gon Jinn is an experienced Jedi who has proven his value to the order in many important missions. In his maturity, however, he remains as headstrong as he was in his youth. When Qui-Gon meets young Anakin Skywalker on Tatooine, the Jedi is convinced that the boy's destiny is linked to the Force.

QUI-GON'S LIGHTSABER

Qui-Gon has built a lightsaber with a highly elaborate internal design. Multiple small power cells are stored in the scalloped handgrip and microscopic circuitry governs the nature of the energy blade.

Qui-Gon believes he has recognized the prophesied individual who will restore harmony to the Force. He takes on the members of the Jedi High Council, including Yoda, who sense danger in the boy.

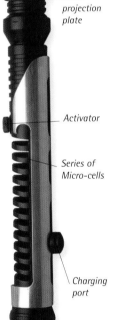

Blade projection plate

Activator

Series of Micro-cells

Charging port

SAMURAI SWORDFIGHT

Two samurai fight with katana, their long fighting swords. These swords were among the finest ever made. Like the Jedi, the samurai had a strict code of behavior.

SAMURAI SWORDS

These Japanese swords are extremely sharp. The short sword was also used for fighting.

Blade is soft iron core covered with layers of steel

Fishskin-covered wooden hilt bound with braid

Lightsaber dueling is taught as part of classical Jedi training – even though it is to be used only in defense.

OBI-WAN KENOBI

Obi-Wan Kenobi has followed a responsible path on his journey to Jedi knighthood as the Padawan apprentice to Qui-Gon Jinn. A serious, quiet man with a dry sense of humor, Obi-Wan feels honored to be Qui-Gon's student, although he worries about his Master's tendency to take risks in defiance of the Council. Obi-Wan is more cautious than his teacher.

Blade modulation circuitry

Blade emitter

Blade length and intensity control

Activator

Internal blade crystals

Handgrip

Single main internal power cell

Charging port

Power cell reserve cap

Long woollen habit

Warm cloak for cold weather

Leather belt

OBI-WAN'S LIGHTSABER

Obi-Wan's lightsaber is similar to Qui-Gon's – apprentices usually build their lightsabers to resemble those of their teachers as a mark of respect. All are hand-built by the initiates themselves, and the exact design details are a matter of individual choice. Optional elements, like blade power, are small and unobtrusive. Like the samurai sword, the Jedi lightsaber is always handled with respect.

ROBES OF THE ORDER
This picture shows the simple habit of the Benedictine monks. Saint Benedict, who founded the order, stated that a monk's clothes should be plain but comfortable.

Obi-Wan Kenobi wears the basic Jedi clothing of belted tunic, travel boots, and robe. It affirms the order's philosophy of simplicity.

Obi-Wan is an exceptional lightsaber duelist and a formidable opponent. Darth Maul fights with inhuman intensity, fueled by the energy of the dark side of the Force. To defeat the hateful Sith Apprentice, Obi-Wan needs a centered awareness, cool concentration, and a deadly aim.

WARRIOR QUEEN

Myths often tell of princesses and queens in distress; in other tales, they are brave warriors. Amidala, ruler of the Naboo people, is both. Her exceptional diplomatic abilities and calm gravity are evident during ceremonial duties. But in the crisis that descends upon her people, it is her courage in the face of adversity that will prove her worth as a warrior companion to her Jedi protectors and as a great queen.

Hand-stitched gold embroidery

While traveling to Coruscant, the disguised Queen is tortured by the replay of a hologram that tells of catastrophic death back on her home planet. Should she return to help or continue on with her mission?

IN DISGUISE

When it becomes necessary to escape from danger or travel incognito, many heroes and princesses assume a disguise. Queen Amidala disguises herself as one of her handmaidens, taking the name Padmé Naberrie. Without her heavy white makeup and formal robes, most people do not give Padmé a second glance, enabling her to see things a queen does not normally see.

The identical hooded dresses and similar appearance of Amidala's handmaidens make it easy for Padmé to appear and disappear quietly from the royal group.

In the assault on her own palace, the Queen fights alongside her troops and Jedi allies to confront the invaders. True to her royal training, she is calm under fire.

THE FOOL

The mythic hero is sometimes accompanied by a foolish companion who turns out to be an unexpected help in a crisis. During the invasion of Naboo, Qui-Gon Jinn rescues the Gungan exile, Jar Jar Binks, who then feels honor-bound to stick with the Jedi for life. Clumsy Jar Jar turns out to be as useful as he is troublesome.

Determined warrior stance

Cesta

Partially retractable eyestalk

JAR JAR THE GENERAL

Much to everyone's surprise and dismay, Jar Jar is made a general in the Gungan Grand Army. He is particularly prone to panic attacks when in danger.

FRIENDLY ALIEN

Like all Gungans, Jar Jar's skeleton is made of cartilage, making him flexible and rubbery. Even his skull and jaws are elastic, giving the simple Gungan a wide range of flexible expressions. Like his body, Jar Jar's character is resilient and able to bend with the changes of fortune.

At first both Jedi Knights are reluctant to have Jar Jar's company, but soon the amphibian proves useful in suggesting an escape plan.

Jar Jar's insatiable curiosity lands him in trouble when he catches his tongue in Anakin's Podracer engine binders.

In her guise as Padmé, Amidala accompanies Qui-Gon Jinn and Jar Jar to Mos Espa to see for herself what's going on. She has doubts about the Jedi plan but cannot reveal her identity.

Electromotive drive fins

Port cargo bubble

GUNGAN CRAFT

A submarine is essential to nagivate the underwater passages connecting Otoh Gunga to the Naboo capital city, Theed. Jar Jar complicates matters by being petrified of the deep-sea creatures.

Organic Gungan design

Spongy kneecaps

Castoff stretchy Gungan trousers

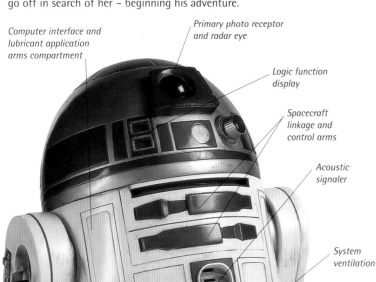

In desperation, Princess Leia programs the droid to record an appeal for help in his memory banks. It is this message that Luke intercepts and causes him to go off in search of her – beginning his adventure.

DROIDS OF DESTINY

The hero's adventure often begins with a message from an unexpected source. The sudden appearance of two droids called R2-D2 and C-3PO with the princess's holographic message marks the starting point of Luke's destiny. The little droid also carries hidden within him the key to the success of Luke's hero task: the secret plans that will help Luke escape from, and ultimately destroy, the Death Star.

At first Luke chooses a different utility droid, but fate intervenes on R2-D2's behalf by causing his red competitor to malfunction. C-3PO puts in a good word for his counterpart and Artoo is bought instead.

Computer interface and lubricant application arms compartment

Primary photo receptor and radar eye

Logic function display

Spacecraft linkage and control arms

Acoustic signaler

System ventilation

Interference pulse stabilizers

Third tread (retractable)

R2-D2

Originally designed as a utility droid, R2-D2 is also a highly useful astromech repair unit. His long history of adventures has given him a distinctly quirky personality and an extraordinary determination to carry out his assigned tasks. Although an interpreter must translate his electronic beeps and whistles for human ears, the droid usually manages to get his points across. Artoo is never reluctant to risk damage or destruction to help his owners accomplish their missions.

MYTHICAL MAILMAN

In his role as messenger of the gods, Hermes had to be cunning, ingenious, knowledgeable, and creative – all characteristics that R2-D2 uses in his efforts to get his mistress Leia's message to Obi-Wan Kenobi.

C-3PO

In a galaxy filled with countless cultures and languages, protocol droids assist their masters in matters of etiquette, custom, and translation, ensuring that intercultural relations proceed peacefully. C-3PO is fluent in over six million forms of communication and has been programed with a strong desire to see things run smoothly. Thrown by R2-D2's mission into a world of adventure, this eccentric character is often overwhelmed by the extraordinary events around him.

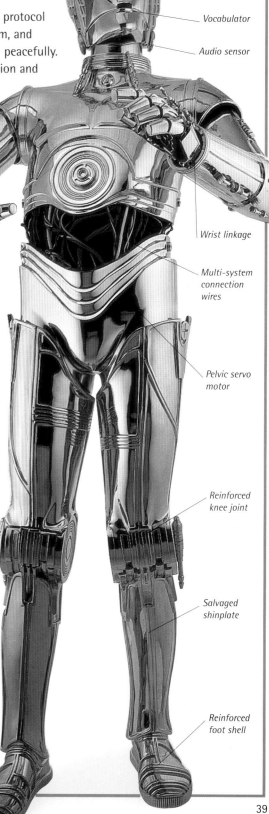

Photoreceptor

Vocabulator

Audio sensor

Wrist linkage

Multi-system connection wires

Pelvic servo motor

Reinforced knee joint

Salvaged shinplate

Reinforced foot shell

An on-board astromech unit is a vital component of the X-wing fighter. Luke chooses to take his trusty R2-D2 in the Rebel attack on the Death Star.

Balance gyro

Vocoder plate

Movement sensor wiring

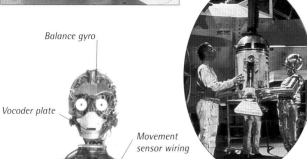

Main power recharge socket

A dedicated droid, C-3PO is frequently damaged in pursuit of his duty, but as he feels no pain, it merely means a spell in the repair shop.

PROTOTYPE C-3PO

When the young Anakin Skywalker finds a broken protocol droid, he keeps it and over the years salvages the parts to restore it. Although he has fixed small electronic devices for some time, this is his first fully functional droid.

Young Anakin has not got the funds to provide the plating to cover the insides, so the early C-3PO looks strangely unfinished.

High-torque knee joint

SEED OF EVIL

Anakin Skywalker's story is a tragic one. As a young boy he has potential and immense gifts but fate has a dark destiny in store for him. Despite support and training from Jedi Knights, hate, fear, and anger eventually turn Anakin to the dark side of the Force and he becomes Darth Vader.

During the invasion of Naboo, Anakin's dream of becoming a fighter pilot comes true. Many years later his flying abilities are put to evil use when, serving the Empire, he becomes the scourge of the Rebels in his lethally agile TIE Advance X1.

Slave's clothing

Anakin Skywalker   Saesee Tiin   Ki-Adi-Mundi   Yoda   Mace Windu   Plo Koon

Anakin's life changes when Jedi Master Qui-Gon Jinn recognizes that the Force is extremely strong in him. With Qui-Gon's support, Anakin finds himself in front of the Jedi High Council on Coruscant being considered for training as a Jedi Knight. Yoda, however, believes that the boy is too old and afraid. Although Qui-Gon will not give up his conviction that Anakin is destined for greatness, the Council at first refuse to accept him. Recently separated from his mother, Anakin is afraid he will lose her. Yoda knows it is dangerous to train a boy so fearful.

Leg wraps keep out sand

EARLY SIGNS

Raised by his mother Shmi, who taught him to believe in himself, Anakin's young life was very hard as a child slave on the desert planet of Tatooine. Yet it made him strong and determined to improve his situation in life. His extraordinary gifts and a natural ability with mechanical devices soon caused him to be noticed by the Jedi order.

Sensing the boy is a threat to the Jedi order, Obi-Wan Kenobi does not want Qui-Gon to train Anakin. After Qui-Gon's death, Obi-Wan has a change of heart and accepts the boy as his own apprentice.

Many years after Anakin has taken the name Darth Vader, Luke Skywalker enters his life. The dark lord immediately senses his son's powers and appeals to Luke to join him on the dark side of the Force, promising that they could rule the galaxy together. Luke has the strength to resist.

DARK LORD

Darth Vader's forbidding appearance is not merely for effect: he is unable to survive without the constant life-support provided by his suit. His injuries occurred in a battle with his one-time teacher, Obi-Wan Kenobi, and much of his body has been replaced with cyborg components. The mask also serves to hide the man within, Anakin Skywalker, the former Jedi Knight.

Vision enhancement receptors

Speech projector and respiratory intake

Control function connectors

Impressed by Vader's abilities, the Emperor favored the dark lord and aided his rise to power as a much-feared military commander in the Imperial Navy.

At the very heart of the second Death Star, Darth Vader and the Emperor attempt to sway Luke to join their evil cause. Despite his horror at what his father has become, Luke is committed to finding redemption for him and gaining freedom for the galaxy.

Darth Vader allows no one to assist him with his accoutrements. In a special isolation chamber, mechanical arms facilitate the removal and replacement of his helmet and mask.

MASK OF FEAR
Japanese samurai armor was designed to protect the whole body, even the face. Like Vader's mask, the samurai's facial armor was intended to strike terror into their opponents.

MORDRED
Deathly figures of evil are common in legend. King Arthur's evil nephew, Mordred, "the black knight," envied Arthur's throne. He waged war on the King using the evil powers of his mother's witchcraft, and plunged the country into civil war.

BRUTAL CRONOS

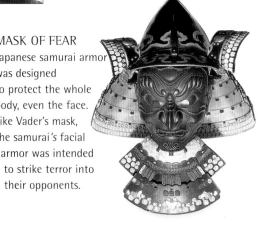

The Greek god Cronos devoured his own children to prevent any of them from succeeding him as leader of the gods. However, his last child, Zeus, was hidden from him and grew up to kill his father. Before he is finally redeemed, Vader would also "devour" his children to ensure the Empire's survival.

IMPERIAL STORMTROOPERS

Imperial Stormtroopers are first-strike units sent into critical combat situations in support of the Imperial Star Fleet and the Imperial Army. Equipped with powerful armaments, they are the most effective troops in the Imperial military, and the most deeply feared opponents of the Rebel fighters.

Stormtrooper armor is impervious to projectile weapons and blast shrapnel. It may be pierced by a direct blaster bolt, but will deflect glancing bolts. Made up of 18 separate plastoid pieces, it is highly durable.

Reinforced helmet

Audio pickup

Air supply nozzles

Manual suit controls

Utility belt

Reinforced alloy plate

Suit systems power cells

Positive grip boots

Holder for horsehair crest.

Deep neck guard to deflect sword strokes.

Upper part of armor attached to lower with bronze hooks.

Armor laced together at the front.

FULL METAL JACKET
Like Stormtrooper armor, this Imperial Roman legionary armor is made of many joining parts. The iron strips are held together by leather straps on the inside. It is flexible but very heavy, and soldiers had to help each other put it on.

Blaster power cell container

Blast energy sink

Helmet computer

Heat dispersion panel

Comlink

STORMTROOPER HELMET
This cut-away shows the comlink and air intake system inside a strormtrooper's helmet.

Sniper position knee protection plate

Setting adjust

Gas cartridge cap

Magnatomic adhesion grip

Safety catch

Accessory mounting rail

Range-finding sight

Heat vents

Cooling fins

Folding stock

STORMTROOPER BLASTER
The standard Imperial sidearm combines excellent range with lethal firepower in a compact design. A standard power cell carries enough energy for 100 shots and the unit features an advanced cooling system for superior performance.

In battle, stormtroopers are trained to ignore casualties within their own ranks. They are never distracted by emotional responses.

Stormtroopers, like Roman legionaries, get used to fighting in the many different terrains and environments of the Empire.

Stormtroopers are sent to crush resistance and do the toughest fighting. Boarding parties are systematic and professional in taking charge of a captured ship.

Often deployed and paraded in huge numbers, stormtrooper legions are drilled to assemble, march, and attack in many tactical formations. Here they are forming a guard of honor to greet the Emperor.

GOTHIC BATTLE GEAR

This 15th-century German armor is made up of many separate steel plates designed to deflect the edges of weapons in hand-to-hand combat. The knight carries an iron mace, which can smash a skull, and a sharp sword for stabbing between an opponent's steel plates. Clashes between such heavily armored warriors could be tiring, bloody, and noisy.

Leather glove inside gauntlet

Mace

FREE FIGHTING

Plate armour is often thought of as clumsy and stiff. In fact, armorers made suits like this so that all the parts moved easily with the body. Sliding rivets and connecting leather straps allowed for free and rapid maneuvering during a fight.

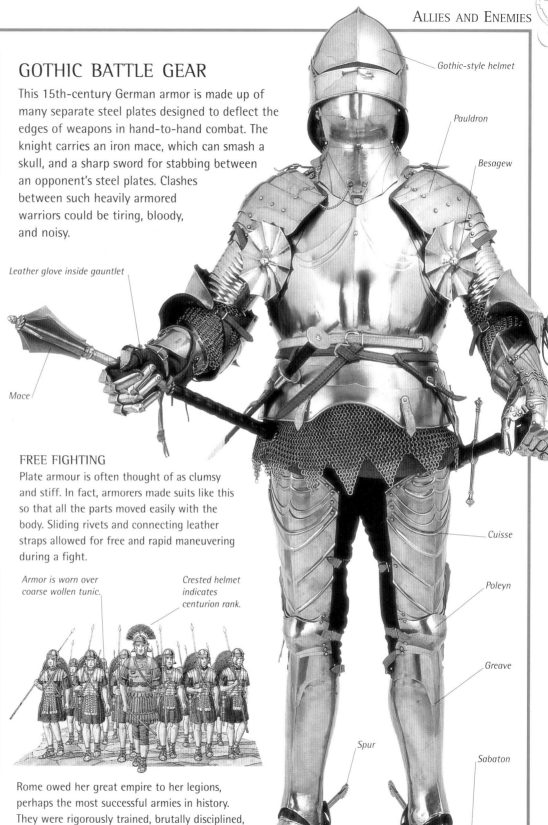

Gothic-style helmet

Pauldron

Besagew

Cuisse

Poleyn

Greave

Spur

Sabaton

Armor is worn over coarse wollen tunic.

Crested helmet indicates centurion rank.

Rome owed her great empire to her legions, perhaps the most successful armies in history. They were rigorously trained, brutally disciplined, and well armed. Barbarian rebels were no match for advancing legionaries, marching in a phalanx.

BATTLE DROIDS

The wealthy Trade Federation has quietly
assembled a massive army of ghostly droid
soldiers to invade the small planet of Naboo.
The arrival of these legions on the friendly
planet heralds the end to an age of peace and
security in the galaxy. Like the skeleton warriors
encountered by the hero Jason during his
adventures with the Argonauts, battle droids
are terrifying for being lifeless and unthinking.

Jason had to kill the many-headed hydra before he
could get to the Golden Fleece. Furious at the
Fleece's theft, the evil king Aeërtes raised a band
of skeletal warriors by planting the hydra's teeth.

Battle droids are carried to strategic positions in
armored MTT tanks. Once deployed, the droids unfold
into symmetrical ranks, ready to advance on the
enemy in tight battle formation. Lacking a brain of
its own, the battle droid is controlled by
a central computer.

BATTLE DROID BLASTER

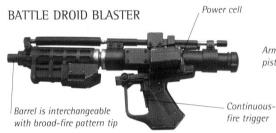

Power cell

Barrel is interchangeable
with broad-fire pattern tip

Continuous-
fire trigger

Although armed with deadly blasters, the battle
droids' firing accuracy is poor because sensory
data is relayed back to the central computer
before the droid is instructed to shoot.

UNFOLDING DROID
Battle droids are designed
to fold up tightly for
efficient storage. 112
droids can be carried in
the special deployment
rack of an MTT.

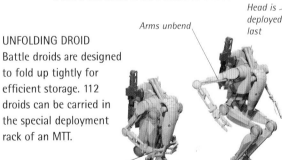

Arms unbend

Head is
deployed
last

Claws grip legs
for stability

Legs fully
upright

The epic film *Spartacus* captures the
awesome spectacle of the Roman army
advancing on rebel forces in a formation
called a phalanx. Infantry marched in a solid
line, presenting long spears from behind
a wall of overlapping shields.
This could be very difficult for
an enemy to penetrate.

The battle droids themselves
march in a unified phalanx,
controlled by the droid
central computer. Their
even-paced advance
penetrates the Gungan
defensive bubble.

General
command
storage

Optical
sensor

Signal boost
power backpack

Arm extension
piston

High torque
motors

Generic feet
can be
replaced
with claws

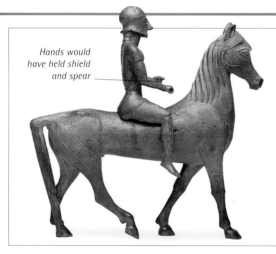

Hands would have held shield and spear

THE STAP

Battle droid scouts sweep through the air on armed Single Trooper Aerial Platforms. The STAP's minimal structure allows it to thread its way through dense forest that would be inaccessible to heavier vehicles like tanks. In warfare, the horse has been used in much the same way. Horses have been of immense military importance. They helped warriors cover difficult ground quickly, and, in combat, horsemen could ride down unprotected foot soldiers. This bronze warrior was made at Taranto, in southern Italy, in about 550 B.C.

Droidekas carry deflector shield generators that can completely repel pistol fire and weaken high-energy rifle bolts. This makes them devastating in combat.

DROIDEKAS

When a droideka is ready to begin an assault, it unfolds and stands on three legs. Its pneumatic arms flex open and its eerie head rises with its enemy-finding sensors ablaze. Powerful twin blasters are built onto its arms. Unlike the lightly built battle droids, every part of a droideka is heavy alloy or armor.

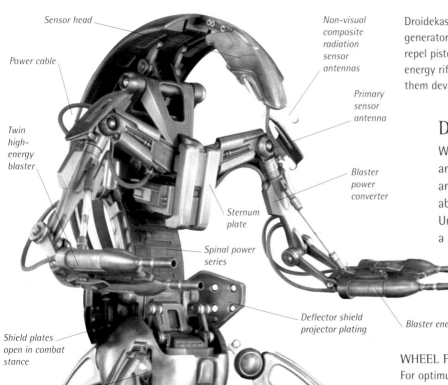

Sensor head

Power cable

Non-visual composite radiation sensor antennas

Primary sensor antenna

Twin high-energy blaster

Blaster power converter

Sternum plate

Spinal power series

Deflector shield projector plating

Blaster energizer

Collimating tip concentrates blaster bolt energy

Shield plates open in combat stance

Hip joint

Case-hardened bronzium armor bulb protects reactor

Legs guide droid

Foot claw designed for hard surfaces

FRONT VIEW

WHEEL FORM

For optimum travel speed, droidekas roll into battle in wheel form.

Sensor head

Sternum plate

Primary rolling surface

Lateral boom for weapon arm

Rear leg

Deflector shield projector flaps

NIGHT OF THE SITH

The Sith Master Darth Sidious sets into motion the final stages of his order's plan to destroy the Jedi. Working patiently, he has extended his power deep into the government. Using his grasp of bureaucracy to stifle justice, he brings about the crisis he needs to make his move.

HIDDEN EVIL

It is on the decisions of the Jedi High Council that the fate of the galaxy will turn as the forces of darkness gather strength on Coruscant. The city is also a hiding place for the unseen Sith. This ancient order has been waiting in the shadows preparing for an era of Sith rule.

KENDO

Sith Apprentice Darth Maul's deadly technique is similar to that used in the martial art of kendo - a form of fencing using wooden swords. Competitors wear elaborate armor, including protective masks, gloves, and breastplates. Very fast reflexes are needed to avoid an opponent's blows.

Sidious has trained one of the most dangerous Sith apprentices in the history of the order. Appearing together in a hologram, they seem like spectres from the mythical Hades.

With his unusual lighsaber, Maul is equal to two Jedi who are unprepared for his powers. Since the Sith had disappeared 1,000 years ago, the order's sudden return surprises Qui-Gon Jinn and Obi-Wan Kenobi.

DARK ORDER

The Sith Order began two millennia ago with a renegade Jedi who sought to use the Force to gain control. Strengthened and twisted by the dark side, the Sith fought each other until just one remained: Darth Bane. Bane remade the Sith as an order that would endure in only two initiates at a time.

Hooded and unseen, Maul prides himself on his abilities as a tracker, and relishes the challenge of difficult assignments given to him by his Sith Master.

PROBE DROID
One of Maul's most useful tools is the "dark eye" probe droid, a device that can be programed to seek out individuals or information.

Transmission antenna

Magnetic imaging device

Scan absorbing stealth shell

Primary photoreceptor

Thermal imager

Levitator

Maul's diabolical appearance recalls the ancient image of a horned demon. This woodcut of the devil dates from the European witch craze of the 17th century, when thousands of people were tried on suspicion of witchcraft and burned at the stake.

MAUL'S LIGHTSABER
Darth Maul has built a double-bladed lightsaber as his primary weapon. Traditionally used only for training, this weapon can be far more dangerous to its wielder than an enemy. In the hands of Darth Maul, however, it becomes a whirling vortex of lethal energy.

Blade modulation control

Control lock

Ribbed handgrip

Heavy-action boots

Blade protection plate

DARTH MAUL
Apprentice to Darth Sidious, Maul is one of the most highly trained Sith in the history of the order. He serves his master obediently, believing that his own time for domination will come. His tattooed face symbolizes his dedication to the dark side.

Vestigial horns

Face tattooes

Gleaming yellow eyes

Beam emitter

Double-bladed lightsaber

Field cloak cut to allow fighting movement.

Lightsaber blade is red due to nature of internal crystals.

www.starwars.com   www.dk.com

PROJECT EDITOR David John
PROJECT ART EDITOR Stefan Morris
MANAGING ART EDITOR Cathy Tincknell
MANAGING EDITOR Joanna Devereux

DESIGNER Gary Hyde
PRODUCTION Carolyn King
PICTURE RESEARCH Angela Anderson
DTP DESIGNER Jill Bunyan

First published in the United States in 1999 by
DK Publishing Limited,
95 Madison Avenue, New York, New York 10016

®, ™, and copyright © 1999 Lucasfilm Ltd.

ISBN 0-7894-5591-9

Acknowledgments

Dorling Kindersley would like to thank:
David West Reynolds, author of the books which appear on the back cover, for
extracts of text; Iain Morris, Sarah Hines Stephens, and Steve Sansweet at
Lucasfilm for additional design, editorial work, and advice on images;
Professor Daithi O'Hogain of University College Dublin for academic advice on
the penportraits of European heroes; Kellogg's for sponsoring the Power of
Myth roadshow; the following team at Megaprint Group: Mary Aiken, Creative
Director of the Power of Myth roadshow, Linda Murray, roadshow Project
Coordinator, Geoff Rayner, Designer of the Power of Myth roadshow, Peter
Aiken, Producer of the Power of Myth roadshow; John Kelly and Guy Harvey
for additional in-house design work; Jacky Jackson, Martin Redfern, and
Simon Beecroft for additional in-house editorial work.

Picture Credits:
Dorling Kindersley would like to thank the following for their kind permission
to reproduce their images:
AGK London: 38 br, Birmingham City Museum and Art Gallery JACKET; 25 tr,
Cameraphoto 27 br, Musee du Louvre/Erich Lessing 25 bc;

Ancient Art & Architecture Collection: JACKET; 41 cb;
Bridgeman Art Library, London/New York: 15 c, 18cr, 21 bc 21 tl, 22 tl,
Biblioteca Nazionale, Turin, Italy, 24bl, Bradford Art Galleries and Museums
13br, City of Edinburgh Museum and Art Galleries, Scotland 19 tl, Oriental
Museum, Durham University 32 br, Phillips International Fine Art Auctioneers
19c, Stapleton Collection 29 cr;
British Museum: 45 tl;
E.T. Archive: 33 bl;
Mary Evans Picture Library: 12 br, 15 tl, 22 cl, 27 bl, 29 tr, 33 tl, Arthur
Rackham Collection 12 cl 16 bl, 19 br;
Fotomas Index: 17 tr;
Michael Holford: 34-35 t;
Kobal Collection: Columbia Pictures 44 tc, Warner Brothers 28 bl, 44 clb;
Sporting Picture (UK) Ltd: 46 c, 46 cl 46 cr;
Nilesh Mistry: JACKET br, 5 bc, 11 bl, 14 bl, 16 bc, 20-21 c, 24 tl, 31 br,
Brian Delf:43 bc
Wallace Collection: 3 tl, 12 l;
Danish National Museum: 4 bc 12 tr